名流詩叢 24

人生襤褸
LIFE'S RAGS

你決定過來
跟我們站在一起支援
我們刻在風中的石頭名字
沿德瑞尼卡路走
即使死後
阿爾貝里亞承載我們重量

〔阿爾巴尼亞〕塞普‧艾默拉甫 (Shaip Emërllahu) ◎著

李魁賢 (Lee Kuei-shien) ◎譯

譯序

李魁賢

　　阿爾巴尼亞人在鄂圖曼土耳其帝國統治時期，要求文化和政治上的自治未成，發展成民族主義運動，追求獨立，終於在1912年11月28日脫離鄂圖曼帝國。由於阿爾巴尼亞人居住散布地區廣，土地又被巴爾幹半島各國分割，獨立後情勢更加複雜。

　　阿爾巴尼亞民族居住土地範圍，目前主要涵蓋阿爾巴尼亞共和國、科索沃、馬其頓西部、塞爾維亞部分地區、蒙特內哥羅南部，以及希臘轄下的伊庇魯斯等地區。因此，阿爾巴尼亞人對國家和民族認同，多少會有不全然一致的情況。在1989年東歐民主自由運動時期，巴爾幹半島各國紛紛尋求獨立自主的大浪潮中，阿爾巴尼亞人反而艱苦備嘗，在塞爾維亞阻擾牽制下受創嚴重，科索沃戰爭延續多年，成為20世紀末最慘烈的世界關心重點之一。

　　台灣對阿爾巴尼亞相當隔閡，我個人對阿爾巴尼亞歷史、文化、文學、詩，所知更是膚淺。2016年5月意外接到馬其頓「奈姆日」國際詩歌節主席塞普‧艾默拉甫（Shaip Emërllahu）邀請書，參加慶祝奈姆‧弗拉舍里（Naim Frashëri）誕生170週年和第20屆「奈姆日」國際詩歌節活動，由於雙慶的特殊意義，今年首創活動範圍涵蓋馬其頓、阿爾巴尼亞共和國和科索沃，同屬阿爾巴尼亞文化圈的三國。我開始注意奈姆‧弗拉舍里的詩創作、復興阿爾巴尼亞文化和語言的志業，從而追求阿爾巴尼亞政治獨立運動的輝煌成果，於是欣然接受邀約。

　　由於「奈姆日」國際詩歌節20年來首度邀請台灣詩人參加，按照個人多年來在國際詩交流活動的作法，儘量爭取有更多名額讓台灣詩人在國際上表現，我希望能給台灣詩人至少五位名額，可惜塞普‧艾默拉甫礙於「奈姆日」國際詩歌節傳統規定，以一國一人為原則，未能答應，後經以本人年歲八十，需有人同行以便照應為理由，破例另邀近年詩創作猛進的陳秀珍出席。

　　為進入阿爾巴尼亞詩壇親歷觀察，不得不對阿爾巴尼亞詩做一些功課，塞普・艾默拉甫也為首次邀請台灣詩人參加，用心對台灣詩進行初步探索，由此契機，彼此以互譯作品做為門檻，做為台灣和阿爾巴尼亞將來持續長程交流的管道。

　　更意外的是，9月初我正在淡水參加福爾摩莎國際詩歌節時，接到塞普・艾默拉甫聯絡，要確認我到達馬其頓班機，準備給我一個驚喜禮物。10日即接到正式通知我，經代表馬其頓、阿爾巴尼亞共和國和科索沃三個國籍的評審委員評審會議結果，以拙詩具有「高度美學和藝術價值」（For high esthetic and artistic values）的理由，決定頒給我2016年奈姆・弗拉舍里文學獎，賦予桂冠詩人榮銜，並聘為詩歌節榮譽委員，將於10月20日開幕時頒贈，另以阿爾巴尼亞文翻譯拙詩15首，登載於大會手冊。

　　我對塞普・艾默拉甫詩回應的翻譯功課，就是這本《人生襤褸》（Life's Rags）詩集。這些詩正如書名所隱喻，以破碎斷片象徵阿爾巴尼亞人生命困境和遭遇，身為台灣人應該容易感同身受，尤其割裂語言表達不可說、不忍說、不明說的人民境遇，社會動蕩和戰亂景象、若隱若現浮出眼前。

「奈姆日」國際詩歌節儀式隆重，啟幕前在放烽炮和少男少女以民俗服裝高舉火炬的陣列前，由泰托沃傑出的女市長托伊達・阿莉菲（Teuta Arifi）、我和身為詩歌節主席的塞普・艾默拉甫，向矗立在泰托沃市文化中心外庭的奈姆・弗拉舍里等身高銅像獻花。五天詩歌節以在文化中心朗誦詩開幕，也在普里什蒂納大學圖書館以朗誦詩閉幕，沒有繁文縟節。

大會另安排參觀泰托沃一處修道院，並越境到科索沃共和國首都普里什蒂納（Pristina）和普里茲倫（Prizren）參觀歷史文化紀念場景，發現科索沃歷經世紀末1999年的戰亂後，社會復興快速，出乎意外，如今已一片繁榮景象，看不出任何戰爭遺跡，人民也都能展向未來努力。

繼此書後，另有《阿爾巴尼亞詩選》計畫進行中，將以含蓋阿爾巴尼亞人的傑出詩篇，不以國籍為限，以求窺視阿爾巴尼亞文化中的詩文學本質。

目次

❶ 人生襤褸

如果明天亮眼的華爾茲

不再演奏

就讓道路向兩側開放

邁步通往過去

只能飽足我們的安慰

正發芽的樹葉

轉變成人生項鍊

誰會責怪

把這些樹葉排成

你頸項的形狀

以此混淆

　　構成人生

與我毫不相干

熱情襤褸

　　人生也

❷ 泰托沃蘋果

經過協調的數世紀

泰托沃修剪澆水

　　　本地蘋果樹

像岩鹽

被你弄髒

因蛆轉成腐敗

你會想爆發

結果

由於吃太多

　　　牙齒麻痺了

1989年，泰托沃

❸ 勝利後復活

—— 致 *Azem Shkreli*

骨骼在勝利轉折中

詩句般散落

受到穩定保護在

稱為科索沃的聖詩裡

　　長鳴鳳凰復活

　　　　勝利後急燥

以其悽美死亡取樂

　　　　用伊利里亞語**

這場勝利的一部分

是阿里‧波多林亞*的復活

1997年5月25日在Tetova

*原註：阿里・波多林亞（Ali Podrimja，1942年生）
　　　是傑出阿爾巴尼亞詩人。

**譯註：伊利里亞語，屬印歐語系，使用位於巴爾幹
　　　半島西部。

❹ 德瑞尼卡路*
——致德瑞尼卡屠殺受害者

每次

你決定過來
跟我們站在一起支援

我們刻在風中的石頭名字
沿德瑞尼卡路走

即使死後
　　阿爾貝里亞**承載我們重量

*德瑞尼卡：1998年在動亂的科索沃區，塞爾維亞警察
　　　　　襲擊普雷卡茲（Prekaz）村莊，造成五十餘
　　　　　位阿爾巴尼亞族村民受害，包含11位 孩童
　　　　　（3到13歲）、11位婦女和5位老人（70歲以
　　　　　上）。

**阿爾貝里亞：是中世紀阿爾巴尼亞人的領土，阿爾巴尼亞
　　　　　　人在巴爾幹半島所認同的居地。

❺ 深夜

陰影隨月亮
來臨
月光騙我們
穿衣
　　在深暗夜裡

人生狂歡晚宴開始
在夜裡最暗時刻
因為那時無火
人生被陰影
　　　擊倒

❻ 天空綻開子彈花

生命的兩把小提琴

在我們正前方被子彈打成碎片

我們偷到琴聲

而生命

生命在泰托沃真美

正如神

祂在夜裡邀我到砲孔

天空綻開子彈花

賦予人民眼睛自由

我們自己目盲的自由眼睛

2001年3月15日泰托沃

❼ 阿爾貝里亞在哪裡

我們渴望的春天

不容走下山來

　　即使霜可帶我們下來也不行

　　兄弟們呀

阿爾貝里亞在哪裡

2001年3月

❽ 絕嶺

——致 Jusuf 和 Bardhosh Gërvalla 以及 Kadri Zeka

絕嶺

我們沒見過

即使

透過判斷之窗

伸長脖子

❾ 十幾年的耳語
——致 *Mulla Jaha*

在「綠區」他們拉出人民鄰居

加以臭罵

        在陽光下

冷風吹拂旗幟

他們相偎取暖

以空包彈遠眺阿爾巴尼亞

毀掉自己的美夢

當特洛伊馬嘶鳴現身

在十幾年的耳語裡變成青銅

春天被他們咳嗽吵醒

❿ 阿爾巴尼亞小徑
——致*Sadudin Gjura*

他追逐小徑陽光
笨腦筋

　　他寬容自己的生命
向前衝留下
　　　　他一直保留的
所有一切

小徑陽光
　　　　離一手之遙

雪
　廣覆他破碎的
夢

走路的方式

透過球體傾聽他

1999年10月14日 在Sadudin墓地

⑪ 偉大日子
—— 致 *Azem Hajdari*

我會很高興

鼓掌歡迎偉大日子

以英雄行為神韻和渴慕

建構我內在

賦於此日光榮動量

我會很高興

以觸覺獻出此偉大日子

並且看看我的足跡

是否留在其前頭

建造或不建造在兒童房間內

我是如此多麼喜愛

即使從墓裡

看或聽

偉大日子到來

（我就靜靜繼續朝永生旅行）

然後悄悄溜走

在我哐啷哐啷的船上

盡此終生

日復一日建造

1998年11月12日 在Trebosh

⑫ 白色山嶺

——致 *Panajot Xhebeliko*

百年殘雪

尚未融化

在Boçari,

　　　　Xhavella

　　　　　　和Katerina山嶺上

南風不吹時

太陽竟迷路了

由於這些伊庇魯斯*山嶺聳立

候鳥只能聽到布穀鳥

伊庇魯斯綠洲呀

這百年殘雪會融化

還是永遠不會

1986年10月在Ioannina

*譯註：伊庇魯斯，橫跨希臘和阿爾巴尼亞的地區。

⑬ 死路

要是你未在人生根底糾纏

狂潮怒浪把你捲走

愛倫坡的烏鴉

會把你的煙囪變成廁所

連鴿子都不飛繞

指著你的

手指

比武器更糟

耗盡你的聲音像夢中

你汗水淋漓

找尋出路

你額頭的惡名標記

令人噁心
像你的征服者笑容
你就是他的穀物

無頭腦方式
始終是無方式頭腦
開發出來的

⑭ 其他時間

即使你換了
　　一百種語音
也不再會受到注意
　　空虛早晨的公雞呀

無人醒來
無

剩餘時間裡
　　鬧鐘在敲打風景

⓯ 人生中你永遠不知道

奔跑丟石頭

變化可能不會太緊跟著你

21世紀明顯來接班

你不知道無法再用

手指記算歲月嗎

你需要十隻手

正如人生中所喜愛

你不可拍打

或許會背叛你

即使光天化日下

急忙向牆壁丟石頭

房子必然是房子

至於人生有誰知道

⑯ 混亂樓梯上的裁判

他試圖仲裁
　　吉力馬札羅風的戰爭
從樓梯追蹤混亂

閃電粉碎了
　　他純白的語彙

⑰ 直到早晨

因為我們夢中有希望無法熟睡

就盲目等待天亮

突然懷疑我們自己

殘廢了

當然

早晨發現我們在笑

天真爛漫在赤道懷抱裡

⑱ 回家的焦慮

當你啟程去旅行
別問
　　你何時回家

只要
拾晨露
洗掉
　　恐懼

1996年夏在Struga

⓳ 微風

銀亮月光夜
拉開

掛在車窗上的
輕飄飄帷幕

我們帶著一些氧氣量

還沒有丟掉

我們只有與神
分享帝國
當怡人的微風
吹動我們腳

輕飄飄帷幕

正掛在車窗上

⑳ 當春天般花開

當我們之間想到遊戲

我心衰弱

春天般花開

妳的唇燦亮成笑容

急冷效果無法抵抗

我有一位學生如此裝模作樣

㉑ 揭開記憶

在卡菲・塔納隘口＊

保留有

滿月的碎影

船清醒駛離時激起

濤浪（和痛苦聲）

　　哈囉

我心中這一聲

揭開此記憶帷幕

2000年在Struga

＊譯註：卡菲・塔納（Qafë Thana）隘口，從馬其
　頓可經此通往阿爾巴尼亞的波格拉德茨
　（Pogradec）、利布拉什德（Librazhd）和
　愛爾巴桑（Elbasan）。

㉒ 歲月洗禮

看歲月多麼艱困

苦難的臉一陣一陣湧出

他們正用歌聲編織五角星

他們血統受洗歲月受洗

只用亂夢的胚芽

只用應許的獨家途徑

從他們髮辮的絲絲縷縷

在手指間失神眼睛的魚骨

在心之心中鴿子咕咕聲

unte paghesont premenit Atit, ...*

以憂傷歲月

以無心歲月

以滿心歲月之名

1989年在Prishtina

*譯註：完整句應為"Unte paghesont prement Atlt et
Birit et Spertit Senit"（以父、子和聖靈之名
為你洗禮）。

㉓ 普里什蒂納大道

大道請原諒

午餐時間

鋪排在悲哀的紅木家具上

連同催淚煙霧

寫在群星裡

昨天你吞噬我們的握手和羞紅的臉

你心裡知道我們上課考試的時間表

你嘲笑我們調情

於菩提樹芳香蔭影下

你稱我們是小孩

或沉醉於青春

看看我們今天為你編造什麼

全心全意

大家手拉手話投機

我們已過度誇大你身體

表現更強壯

直到深夜

我們歌聲繼續搖你入眠

更勝於月亮

消磨掉我們的臉

即使我們嘴唇

似黃昏火熱

即使我們的語音

像子彈沉落

我們悲歡的大道

1990年1月24日在晉里什蒂納（譯註：科索沃共和國首都）。

㉔ 我的世代

即使此刻

你是用母乳餵養

頭髮也都灰白

我的世代呀

　　你們的命運是什麼

㉕ 我們去哪裡

夜晚尾端
停下來招待蟋蟀

早晨樹葉
氣炸了

此時我們去哪裡？！

1994年

26 朝陽走了

我們起立
　　觸摸早晨

黑夜尾巴
拍打
　　我們腳下泥土

朝陽
　　來了又走了

如今……

㉗ 我們不在乎

我們自己付出

　　　　　那麼多

給要奉獻的對象後

我們太平門在拉長的夜遠方

在如今變成異邦

倒下者冷了

我們不在乎

靠不住的王座給我們夠啦

我們就要吃貪婪的臉

㉘ 奧阿尼姆在睡覺

在鼓手

　　前導下

奧阿尼姆*

　　在別地方睡著了

他們不知所措

　　即使在早晨

*奧阿尼姆（Oaneum）是泰托沃市（Tetova City）的伊利里亞語名稱。

㉙ 夢的恍惚

在公雞報曉的方向
我們的夢凍結了

對每一世代
我說了
一遍又一遍

兒童聆聽
懵懵懂懂
我們不知道
他們聽到什麼

我們也不知道

我們祖先

是否能搞清楚

如果他們活

在今世

㉚ 空虛早晨的郵差

當聲明的時間
變成老套

我不想知道
這種熱情是否
能保持
　　　其強度

我對贏家
　　不予評論

空虛的早晨
郵差
　　得其門而入

㉛ 破碎計畫

　　　　甚至當聖先知

　　　　　　放棄他們生命時

　　　　我離開

　　　　我離開死亡

　　　　然而

　　　　雖然死亡

　　　　　　　　死

　　　　　　　猶如生

　　　　在空虛的早晨

　　　　我甚至不喝

　　　　不可或缺的咖啡

　　　　計畫以破碎結束

我也是

　　　　完全徒勞

我的計畫

　　　　我始終試圖

把我的生命建構

死亡

　　　　追求死亡

我的生命計畫

繼續

　　　　永久

　　　　把我自己拼在一起

㉜ 爭論告終

那些還沒到過

克魯亞城堡*的人都在

「滿嘴阿爾巴尼亞」**耳語

他們沒錯

大時代的反對者

已死久矣

1991年1月1日 在Kruja

*譯註：克魯亞，阿爾巴尼亞北方小鎮，古堡矗立在
　　　山岡上，內關斯坎德伯格博物館。
**原註：此意象襲自「滿嘴麵包」。

㉝ 即使你的微笑被監視

你在1937年希特勒崛起的

法西斯主義談判中有罪嗎

　　　　　　Katarzyna

沒人可抵擋

你十七歲的笑容

即使被監視

未來會向你喝采

把你養成最優秀人才

笑聲更宏亮

即使德國人已拆掉柏林圍牆

即使奧德奈塞線*繼起

卡塔濟納呀，繼續跳那狂野黏巴達舞吧

因為柏林‘37年計畫會失敗

柏林1878年計畫也是

錫隆納葛拉仍然是

　　　　　錫隆納葛拉**

而我還是一個我

　　　　*譯註：奧德奈塞線（Oder-Neisse），波蘭與前東德
　　　　　　　間的臨時疆界。
　　　　**原註：錫隆納葛拉（Zielona Góra），德文名
　　　　　　　Grünberg in Schleisen，是波蘭西部城市。

❸❹ 阿爾巴尼亞

墳墓的地理
無法保障
　　你高升

全然徒勞

㉟ 自我犧牲

幾乎黎明時

舊年逝新年生

他們急急忙忙砌牆

始終有惡名

他們說

我們的墓地不能延伸

超出陰影界線

遠離惡夢

我們寧願旅行讓夢活在

牆外

在最幸福的太陽王國裡

36 阿爾巴尼亞馬拉松

我要

進入

地拉那*

搶先

在

斯巴達馬拉松選手

進入雅典之前

那天我會徒步

我會

帶來消息

中世紀

已告瓦解

我會質疑馬拉松死亡

切望構想

久待的花環

隨後落在

我國土

阿爾巴尼亞馬拉松

來啦而且在這邊

受到歡迎

*譯註：地拉那市（Tiranë），阿爾巴尼亞共和國首都。

關於詩人

　　塞普・艾默拉甫，1962年生於馬其頓泰托沃近郊的特雷玻斯村（Trebosh）。在科索沃的普里什蒂納大學完成阿爾巴尼亞語文學位，擔任過報紙《Flaka》記者和文化編輯，現為泰托沃「奈姆日」（Ditet e Naimi）國際詩歌節主席。參加過哥倫比亞、愛爾蘭、突尼西亞、波蘭、克羅埃西亞、羅馬尼亞、保加利亞、土耳其等國舉辦國際詩歌節，榮獲多項國內和國際文學獎。

出版詩集有《歲月洗禮》（Pagëzimi i viteve，地拉那市奈姆・弗拉舍里出版書房，1994）、《破碎計畫》（Projekti i thyer，斯科普耶市阿爾巴尼亞作家協會，1991）、《小小死神》（Vdekja e paktë，斯科普耶市Flaka出版部，2001）。

2001年保加利亞東西文化學術院（Akademia Orient – Oksident）為他出版阿爾巴尼亞和羅馬尼亞雙語詩集《Vdekja e paktë – Putina moarte》。2000年出版合著阿英雙語詩集《我們作證》（…edhe ne dëshmojnë / We witness，奈姆・弗拉謝里出版書房），見證科索沃屠殺事件。2004年克羅埃西亞筆會和克羅埃西亞作家協會出版其克阿雙語《詩集》。2004年斯科普耶市Feniks出版書房出版其詩選集《Dvorski son》。

塞普・艾默拉甫的詩被譯成法文、英文、希伯來文、西班牙文、阿拉伯文、羅馬尼亞文、波蘭文、克羅埃西亞文、和馬其頓文，本書為首譯華文。

關於漢語譯者

　　李魁賢，1937年生，1953年開始發表詩作，曾任台灣筆會會長，國家文化藝術基金會董事長。現任世界詩人運動組織（Movimiento Poetas del Mundo）副會長。詩被譯成各種語文在日本、韓國、加拿大、紐西蘭、荷蘭、南斯拉夫、羅馬尼亞、印度、希臘、美國、西班牙、巴西、蒙古、俄羅斯、古巴、智利、尼加拉瓜、孟加拉、馬其頓、土耳其、波蘭等國發表。

　　出版著作包括《李魁賢詩集》全6冊、《李魁賢文集》全10冊、《李魁賢譯詩集》全8冊、翻譯《歐洲經典詩選》全25冊、《名流詩叢》24冊、《人生拼圖──李魁賢回憶錄》，及其他共二百本。英譯詩集有《愛是我的信仰》、《溫柔的美感》、《島與島之間》、《黃昏時刻》和《存在或不存在》。《黃昏時刻》共有英文、蒙古文、羅馬尼亞文、俄文、西班牙文、法文、韓文、孟加拉文和阿爾巴尼亞文譯本。

曾獲韓國亞洲詩人貢獻獎、榮後台灣詩獎、賴和文學獎、行政院文化獎、印度麥氏學會詩人獎、吳三連獎新詩獎、台灣新文學貢獻獎、蒙古文化基金會文化名人獎牌和詩人獎章、蒙古建國八百週年成吉思汗金牌、成吉思汗大學金質獎章和蒙古作家聯盟推廣蒙古文學貢獻獎、真理大學台灣文學家牛津獎、韓國高麗文學獎、孟加拉卡塔克文學獎、馬其頓奈姆・弗拉舍里文學獎。

❶ *LIFE'S RAGS*

if tomorrow the waltz of glowing eyes

won't be played

let the road open to both sides

stepping through to the past

feeds only our consolation

the leaf of what's to come

turns into a necklace of life

who's to blame

for this mounting of leaves

in the shape of your neck

while I have nothing to do

with this confusion

      constituting life

passionate rags

      life

❷ *THE APPLES OF TETOVA*

through the concerted centuries

Tetova pruned and watered

           its own apple trees

like rock salt

you'll want to burst

when you spot them turned rotten

from maggots

in the end

they've eaten so much

           their teeth went numb

Tetova, 1989

❸ REBORN AFTER THE VICTORY

For Azem Shkreli

in the turns bones take through history

verse-like and scattered

guarded steadily

in the psalm named Kosovo

      the long-winded phoenix was reborn

           eager after its victory

to make fun of his charming death

           in Illyrian

one portion of this victory

is reborn as Ali Podrimja

Tetova, 25 May 1997

Ali Podrimja (born 1942) is a distinguished
Albanian poet.

❹ *DRENICA ROAD*

To the victims of the massacre of Drenica

each time

you decide to cross over
to stand all of us back up

along Drenica Road
walking our stone names carved in air

even after death

      Arbëria bears our weight

Drenica: In 1998, over fifty ethnic Albanian villagers, including 11 children (from 3 to 10 years old), 11 women and 5 old people (above 70), were victims of the Serb police attack on the village of Prekaz, in the troubled Kosova region of Drenicë.

Arbëria is a patronymic by which are identified all the territories and lands inhabited by Albanians in the Balkans. Arbëria is the name of Albanian territories in the Middle Ages.

❺ *DEEP NIGHT*

shadows had come

with the moon

and its light deceived us

clothed

       in night's deep dark

life's orgy began

it was the darkest time of night

since there was no fire

life got knocked over

       by its shadow

❻ THE SKY BLOOMED WITH BULLET FLOWERS

two violins of life

were torn to pieces by bullets right in front of us

and we stole their sound

and life

life was beautiful above Tetova

just as God is

He invited me at night to the embrasure

when the sky bloomed with bullet flowers

it gave freedom to the eyes of our people

freedom-eyes we ourselves blinded

Tetova, 15 March 2001

❼ WHERE IS ARBËRIA

the spring we longed for

wasn't allowed to step down the mountains

         not even the frost can bring us down

        o brothers

where is Arbëria

March 2001

❽ *SUMMITS*

For Jusuf and Bardhosh Gërvalla and Kadri Zeka

The summits

never appear to us

not ever

through the windows of our judgments

with their craned necks

❾ *WHISPERS OF A DOZEN YEARS*

For Mulla Jaha

in the "green zone" they pulled out a neighborhood of people

all chewed up

        before sunlight

when the cold winds blew the flag

they warmed themselves in

with their blank stares across Albania

spoiling their dream

when a nickering Trojan horse appeared

they turned into bronze in a dozen year's whisper

spring awoke from their cough

⑩ *PATHWAY OF ALBANIA*

To Sadudin Gjura

he chased pathway's sun

awkward thought

    he was his forgiven life

he rushed to leave behind

            all he had

he kept leaving

pathway's sun

        was a hand-width away

snow

    spread wide his tattered

dream

the way of walking

listened to him through the spheres

Sadudin's Grave, 14.X.1999

⓫ *THE GREAT DAY*

For Azem Hajdari

I would very much like

to applaud the Great Day

with the verve of heroic deeds and longing

built up inside me

giving this day glorious momentum

I would very much like

to consecrate this Great Day with a touch

and to see whether my footprints

on its forehead

built or did not build into a nest for the children

so very much I'd love

even from the grave

to see or hear

the Great Day coming

(and then quietly continue my journey toward aeon)

and then slip off quietly

in my clanking boat

built day by day

in this lifetime

Trebosh, 12 November 1998

⑫ *WHITE SUMMITS*

For Panajot Xhebeliko

the hundred-year-old snow

has not yet melted

over Boçari,

      Xhavella

           And Katerina summits

the sun mistook its way

when the south wind didn't blow

since these Epirus summits rose up

the migratory birds heard only the cuckoo

o Epirus Oases

will this hundred-year-old snow melt

or not ever

Ioannina, October 1986

⓭ *DEAD END*

if you're not tangled in life's roots

the furious waves wash you away

Edgar Allan Poe's raven

turns your chimney into a toilet

doves don't even fly around

the finger that points

at you

is worse than weapons

it exhausts your voice as in a dream

and you drown in sweat

looking for a way out

a notorious brand on your forehead

nauseating

like the smile of your conqueror

you're his grist

the headless ways

are always exploited

by wayless heads

⑭ OTHER TIME

even if you changed

one hundred voices

you wouldn't be noticed anymore

o rooster of empty mornings

nobody wakes up

no

in the remaining hours

alarm clocks hit the scene

⓯ *YOU NEVER KNOW IN LIFE*

run throw a stone

may the changes not follow you too closely

the 21st century is successor of the obvious

don't you see you can no longer

count the years on your fingers

you need ten hands

that's what life's like

you can't beat it

perhaps it will betray you

even in broad daylight

hurry throw a stone at the wall

the house has to be the house

as for life one never knows

16 *THE REFEREE ON THE STAIRS OF CHAOS*

he tried to arbitrate

     the wars of the winds of Kilimanjaro

from the stairway tracing the chaos

lightning shattered

     his lily-white vocabulary

⑰ *UNTIL MORNING*

because we had hope in a dream we couldn't sleep

and went blind waiting for its light

and snapped out of it wondering about ourselves

crippled

of course

morning found us smiling

artless in the equator's arms

⑱ *ANXIETY OF RETURNING*

when you set off on a journey

don't ask

   when you'll return

it's enough

to catch the morning dew

to wash away

   that fear

Struga, summer 1996

⑲ *BREEZE*

a silvery moonlit night

sprung open

over the car windows hung

vaporous curtains

we had with us some oxygen rations

we hadn't given up

we shared our Empire

only with God

when a delightful breeze

shook us to our feet

vaporous curtains

were hanging over the car windows

⑳ WHEN IT BLOSSOMS SPRING-LIKE

when a game came up between us

and my heart weakened

spring - like into blossoms

your lips glossed into a smile

a chilling effect impossible to resist

I have a student's take on this

㉑ *OPENING A MEMORY*

in Qafë Thana Pass

there remained

the broken shadow of the full moon

the harsh wave of a ship's departure

(and a painful sound) in its wake

hello

the one in my heart

opened the curtain of this memory

Struga, 2000

㉒ *BAPTISM OF THE YEARS*

look how the years are strenuous

faces of the needy pour out

row upon row they're weaving their song into a pentagram

their strains are baptized the years are baptized

only with the germ of a disturbing dream

only with the path of a promising solo

from the strands of their braided hair

between their fingers fish-bones of an exhausted eye

in the heart of the heart the cooing of doves

unte paghesont premenit Atit,...

the names of years with grief

years of names without heart

years full of hearts

Prishtina, 1989

㉓ PRISHTINA AVENUE

forgive me Avenue

this lunchtime

laid out on sorrow's mahogany

together with lachrymatory smoke

written in the stars

yesterday you ate our handshakes and blushing faces

you knew by heart our schedule of lectures and exams

you laughed at our flirtations

in the fragrance and shadow of a lime tree

you called us children

or drunk with youth

look what we've cooked up for you today

head over heels

all hand in hand or word in word

we have exaggerated your body

to appear stronger

until the late hours

our song continuously cradles you

better than the moon

it wears our faces

even when our lips

are burnt like the dusk

even when our voice

descends like a bullet

Avenue of our joys and sorrows

Prishtina, 24 January 1990

㉔ *MY GENERATION*

even now

as you are breastfed

your hair grizzles

oh my Generation

    what is your destiny

㉕ *WHERE ARE WE GOING*

the tail-end of night

stayed to host crickets

the morning leaf

exploded in anger

where are we going now?!

1994

㉖ THE MORNING SUN PASSING

we stood up

      to touch the morning

night's tail

swiped

      the soil from under our feet

the morning sun

      came and went

now…

㉗ *WE DON'T CARE*

after we paid ourselves

                    so much

to whom shall we dedicate

our exit beyond the drawn out nights

when the fallen ones are cold

from the now foreign land

we don't care

for us enough of that questionable throne

we'll eat the gloating face

㉘ OANEUM'S SLEEPING

under the vanguard

     of the drummers

Oaneum

     is somewhere else asleep

they have bewildered

     even his morning

       *Oaneum: Illyrian name of Tetova City

㉙ THE STUPOR OF THE DREAM

in the direction of the morning rooster's crow

our dream freezes

I told it

over and over

to every generation

the children

listened in a daze

we couldn't tell

what they heard

nor could we tell

if it was spoiled

on our ancestors

where they live

this one time

㉚ *EMPTY MORNING MESSANGERS*

when the time of declarations

becomes old-fashioned

I won't know

if this kind of passion

will keep

       its intensity

I abstain from

       comment on the winner

empty mornings

the messengers

       come through its door

㉛ *BROKEN PROJECT*

even when the holy prophets

        abandoned their lives

I leave

I leave death

nonetheless

though death

        death

        makes it look like life

in empty mornings

I didn't even drink

my much-needed cup of coffee

the *Project* ended up broken

so was I

      entirely in vain

me-project

      all the time I try

to build my life

death

      chases death

me-project-life

continually

      permanently

      I piece myself together

32 THE DISPUTERS ARE DEAD

all those

who haven't been to Kruja Castle

whisper "*Albania a mouthful*"

they're right

the opponents of the Great Year

have died a long time ago

Kruja, 1ˢᵗ January 1991

* Albania a mouthful, the image here as a mouthful
of bread.

33 *EVEN IF YOUR SMILE IS SPIED UPON*

are you guilty of the bargaining of 1937

of the fascism that brought forth Hitler,

Katarzyna

nobody can subdue

your 17 year-old smile

even if it is spied upon

the future world applauds you

brings you up with the greatest finesse

laugh louder

even when the Germans tear down the Berlin Wall

even when "Oder-Neisse" comes up

Katarzyna, keep dancing that wild lambada

because the '37 plan of Berlin will fail

and so will the 1878's plan of Berlin

Zielona Gora will remain

               Zielona Gora

and I the one I am

          Zielona Góra (German: Grünberg in Schleisen)
          is a city in western Poland.

 *ALBANIA*

the geography of graves

doesn't secure your

      ascension

all's in vain

㉟ *SELF-SACRIFICE*

Almost at dawn

The old year dying new year cradling

They hurried to build walls

All through the name

They said

Our graveyards won't stretch

Beyond the border of shadow

Distant from nightmares

Traveling we preferred to live our dream

Outside walls

In the kingdom of the happiest sun

36 *ALBANIAN MARATHON*

I will

enter in

Tirana

before

than

the Spartan marathoner

entered in Athens

I will walk on that day

when I will

bring the news

that the Middle Age

has fallen

I will challenge the marathon death

the great thirst for contemplating

the long awaited wreath

as it comes after

upon my land

the Albanian marathon

comes and is provoked

on this side

English versions by Craig Czury and Elvana Zaimi - Tufa

About the Poet

Shaip Emërllahu was born in 1962 in the village of Trebosh near Tetova, Macedonia. He completed his Philological Degree of Albanian Language and Literature at Prishtina University in Kosovo. Director of the International Poetry Festival "Ditet e Naimit", Tetova, he has worked as a journalist and culture editor for the newspaper "Flaka".

Emërllahu has participated in international and national poetry festivals in Columbia, Ireland, Tunisia, Poland, Croatia, Romania, Bulgaria, Turkey... He has been awarded with many national and international literary prizes.

He has published the poetry volumes "Pagëzimi i viteve" (Baptism of the Years) in the publishing house "Naim Frashëri", Tirana, 1994, "Projekti i thyer" (Broken Project), Albanian Writers' Association, Skopje, 1997, "Vdekja e paktë" (Little Death) in the edition "Flaka", Skopje, 2001. In 2001, "Akademia Orient – Oksident" in Bucharest, published in Albanian and Romanian his poetry book "Vdekja e paktë – Putina moarte". In 2000, he published as a co-author the book about testimonies of the massacres in Kosovo "···edhe ne dëshmojnë / We witness", publishing house "Ditet e Naimit" (in Albanian and English). In 2004, the Croatian PEN and the Croatian Writers' Association published his bilingual Croatian-

Albanian book with the title "Poezi". In 2004, the publishing house "Feniks" in Skopje published his book with selected poems "Dvorski son".

Emërllahu's work has been translated into French, English, Hebrew, Spanish, Arabic, Romanian, Polish, Croatian and Macedonian.

About the Chinese Translator

Lee Kuei-shien (b. 1937) began to write poems in 1953, was elected as President of Taiwan P.E.N., and served as chairman of National Culture and Arts Foundation. At present he is the Vice President of Movimiento Poetas del Mundo. His poems have been translated and published in Japan, Korea, Canada, New Zealand, Netherlands, Yugoslavia, Romania, India, Greece, USA, Spain, Brazil, Mongolia, Russia, Cuba, Chile,

Nicaragua, Bangladesh, Macedonia, Turkey and Poland.

Published works include "Collected Poems" in six volumes, "Collected Essays" in ten volumes, "Translated Poems" in eight volumes, "Anthology of European Poetry" in 25 volumes and "Elite Poetry Series" in 24 volumes, "Jigsaw Puzzle of Life, memoir of Lee Kuei-shien" and others about 200 books in total. His poems in English translation editions include "Love is my Faith", "Beauty of Tenderness", "Between Islands", "The Hour of Twilight" and "Existence or Non-Existence". The book "The Hour of Twilight" has been translated into English, Mongol, Romanian, Russian, Spanish, French, Korean, Bengali and Albanian languages.

Awarded with Merit of Asian Poet, Korea, Rong-hou Taiwanese Poet Prize, Lai Ho Literature Prize and Premier Culture Prize. He also received the Michael Madhusudan Academy Poet Award, Wu San-lien Prize in Literature, Poet Medal from Mongolian Cultural Foundation, Chinggis

Khaan Golden Medal for 800 Anniversary of Mongolian State, Oxford Award for Taiwan Writers, Prize of Corea Literature of Korea, Kathak Literary Award of Bangladesh and Literary Prize "Naim Frashëri" of Macedonia.

Contents

語言文學類　PG1723　名流詩叢24

人生襤褸
LIFE'S RAGS

原　　著 / 塞普・艾默拉甫（Shaip Emërllahu）
譯　　者 / 李魁賢（Lee Kuei-shien）
責任編輯 / 林昕平
圖文排版 / 莊皓云
封面設計 / 葉力安

發 行 人 / 宋政坤
法律顧問 / 毛國樑　律師
出版發行 / 秀威資訊科技股份有限公司
　　　　　114台北市內湖區瑞光路76巷65號1樓
　　　　　電話：+886-2-2796-3638　傳真：+886-2-2796-1377
　　　　　http://www.showwe.com.tw
劃撥帳號 / 19563868　戶名：秀威資訊科技股份有限公司
　　　　　讀者服務信箱：service@showwe.com.tw
展售門市 / 國家書店（松江門市）
　　　　　104台北市中山區松江路209號1樓
　　　　　電話：+886-2-2518-0207　傳真：+886-2-2518-0778
網路訂購 / 秀威網路書店：http://www.bodbooks.com.tw
　　　　　國家網路書店：http://www.govbooks.com.tw

2017年2月　BOD一版
定價：200元
版權所有　翻印必究
本書如有缺頁、破損或裝訂錯誤，請寄回更換

國家圖書館出版品預行編目

人生襤褸 / 塞普‧艾默拉甫（Shaip Emërll）著；李
魁賢（Lee Kuei-shien）譯. -- 一版. -- 臺北市：
秀威資訊科技, 2017.02
　　面；　　公分. -- (語言文學類；PG1723)(名流
詩叢；24)
　　BOD版
　　譯自：Life's rags
　　ISBN 978-986-326-401-9(平裝)

883.451   105024749

讀者回函卡

感謝您購買本書，為提升服務品質，請填妥以下資料，將讀者回函卡直接寄
回或傳真本公司，收到您的寶貴意見後，我們會收藏記錄及檢討，謝謝！
如您需要了解本公司最新出版書目、購書優惠或企劃活動，歡迎您上網查詢
或下載相關資料：http:// www.showwe.com.tw

您購買的書名：＿＿＿＿＿＿＿＿＿＿＿＿＿＿＿＿＿＿＿＿＿＿＿＿

出生日期：＿＿＿＿＿＿年＿＿＿＿＿＿月＿＿＿＿＿日

學歷：□高中 (含) 以下　　□大專　　□研究所 (含) 以上

職業：□製造業　□金融業　□資訊業　□軍警　□傳播業　□自由業
　　　□服務業　□公務員　□教職　　□學生　□家管　□其它＿＿＿

購書地點：□網路書店　□實體書店　□書展　□郵購　□贈閱　□其他

您從何得知本書的消息？

　　□網路書店　□實體書店　□網路搜尋　□電子報　□書訊　□雜誌

　　□傳播媒體　□親友推薦　□網站推薦　□部落格　□其他＿＿＿＿＿

您對本書的評價：(請填代號　1.非常滿意　2.滿意　3.尚可　4.再改進)

　　封面設計＿＿＿　版面編排＿＿＿　內容＿＿＿　文／譯筆＿＿＿　價格＿＿＿

讀完書後您覺得：

　　□很有收穫　□有收穫　□收穫不多　□沒收穫

對我們的建議：＿＿＿＿＿＿＿＿＿＿＿＿＿＿＿＿＿＿＿＿＿＿＿＿

＿＿＿＿＿＿＿＿＿＿＿＿＿＿＿＿＿＿＿＿＿＿＿＿＿＿＿＿＿＿＿＿

＿＿＿＿＿＿＿＿＿＿＿＿＿＿＿＿＿＿＿＿＿＿＿＿＿＿＿＿＿＿＿＿

＿＿＿＿＿＿＿＿＿＿＿＿＿＿＿＿＿＿＿＿＿＿＿＿＿＿＿＿＿＿＿＿

11466
台北市內湖區瑞光路 76 巷 65 號 1 樓
秀威資訊科技股份有限公司 　　收
BOD 數位出版事業部

....

（請沿線對折寄回，謝謝！）

姓　　名：＿＿＿＿＿＿＿＿　年齡：＿＿＿＿　性別：□女　□男

郵遞區號：□□□□□

地　　址：＿＿＿＿＿＿＿＿＿＿＿＿＿＿＿＿＿＿＿＿

聯絡電話：(日)＿＿＿＿＿＿＿＿　(夜)＿＿＿＿＿＿＿＿

E-mail：＿＿＿＿＿＿＿＿＿＿＿＿＿＿＿＿＿＿